E
CU

Curious George goes
hiking

DATE DUE			
JY 29 '92	AUG 11 '90	SEP 2 6 '95	3
OC 15 '92	OCT 27 '94	NOV 2 '95	
FE 2 '93	NOV 30 '94	NOV 1 3 '95	
AP 8 '93	JAN 04 '95	JAN 1 2 '96	3
JE 7 '93	JAN 2 6 '95	AR 2 2 '96	
FEB 19 '94	FEB 1 0 '95	MAY 1 6 '96	APR 0 9 '97
MAR 21 '94	MAR 30 '95	JUN 0 6 '96	JUN 1 1 '97
APR 25 '94	MAY 1 6 '95	JUN 2 6 '96	JUN 25 '97
MAY 23 '94	JUN 0 1 '95	AUG 0 2 '96	JUL 23 '97
JUN 18 '94	JUN 0 1 '95	SEP 1 3 '96	AUG 1 4 '97
AUG 8 '94	JUL 2 9 '95	DEC 2 6 '96	19 '97

FEB 04 '98

Curious George®

GOES HIKING

Adapted from the Curious George film series
edited by Margret Rey and Alan J. Shalleck

1 9 8 5

Houghton Mifflin Company Boston

Library of Congress Cataloging in Publication Data
Main entry under title:

Curious George goes hiking.

   "Adapted from the Curious George film series."
   Summary: Curious George distresses his companions
when he loses the picnic food but makes them happy
again when he finds their way back to civilization.
   1. Children's stories, American. [1. Hiking—
Fiction. 2. Monkeys—Fiction] I. Rey, Margret.
II. Shalleck, Alan J. III. Curious George goes hiking (Motion picture)
PZ7.C9214   1985   [E]   85-2433
ISBN 0-395-39038-9

Printed in Japan

DNP   10   9   8   7   6   5   4   3   2   1

"Here are your friends,
Ted and Suzie," said the man with the
yellow hat. Today George was going on a hike.

"I'll pick you up later. Have a good time but don't get into trouble."

"George, you carry this bag of marshmallows," said Suzie.

"Let's go," said Ted, and they started down the trail.

"Look! There's a cardinal," whispered Ted.

The cardinal landed on a rock. George tiptoed closer
to get a better look.

But he tripped on a branch and
dropped the bag of marshmallows.

The bag hit a sharp rock and split wide open.

"Come on, George, we're waiting for you," Suzie shouted.

George picked up the broken bag and
hurried after his friends.

Not far down the trail, they saw a deer.
"Look!" Ted called.

The three of them ran after it.

George did not notice the rip in the bag.

While Ted, Suzie, and George
ran through the woods the marshmallows
fell out one by one.

They chased the deer across a little brook.
But the deer was too fast for them.

"I'm tired," said Ted. "Let's stop."

"I'm hungry," said Suzie. "Let's eat the marshmallows."
"Let me have the bag, George," said Ted.

George handed the bag to Ted, but the bag was empty.
Not a single marshmallow was left.

Ted was angry. "Look what you've done!" he shouted.
"Now we have nothing to eat."

George started to cry. "We'd better take you home," said Suzie.

"Does anyone know where we are?" asked Ted. They
had chased the deer so far that they had lost their way.

Ted and Suzie were scared. "It's getting late," said Ted.
"What are we going to do?" cried Suzie. "We're lost."

But George knew what to do! He took Ted and Suzie by the hand

and led them along the path of the spilled marshmallows.
"We can follow the marshmallows right back to where we came
from!" Ted said.

And that's what they did, all the way back to where the
man with the yellow hat was waiting for them. "I'm so
glad to see you," he said. "I was getting worried."

"We were lost," said Suzie, "but George saved the day."

"Good for you, George," said the man. "Let's celebrate.
We'll toast another bag of marshmallows in our fireplace at home."

And that's what they did.